DRIVING HER WILD

MARIAH ANKENMAN

CONTENTS

COPYRIGHT

Edited by P.K.

DEDICATION

To David Rose
"I like the wine not the label"
Same.

CONTENT WARNING

Content Warning

Driving Her Wild is a fun, open door steamy romance with a happy ending, but there are a few on page depictions that may be triggering for some readers. Discussions of homophobic parents, family estrangement, and an on-page car accident (no injuries to any people, just the car). Please read with care.

CHAPTER 1

"*I*'m telling you, the real money is in plastic surgery. You gotta look into it."

Jodie Saunders did her best to hold the smile on her face, but her cheeks hurt like heck from the three-hour flight sitting next to Mr. Know-it-all. The second she told her seatmate she was a veterinarian he launched into a long diatribe about how animal medicine had no money in it and she should switch to the glamorous and high paying world of fake boobs and nose jobs.

As if it was that easy to switch. Like she hadn't spent the past eight years studying for a specific degree. Did Douchebag McGee even realize it was harder to get into veterinary school than medical school? It might not be as glamorous or able to fund a high-flying lifestyle, but she loved animals, and she was excited to start her internship.

"Thank you, but I prefer working with animals."

Her seatmate—who failed to introduce himself before he started giving her unwanted life advice—stared at her like she'd grown an extra head. She held back a sigh, used to this reaction from people.

"But they scratch and bite and shit all over everything," he said with a look of horror.

She could point out that human patients did the same thing, but instead she shrugged, willing the captain to turn off the seatbelt sign now that they landed so she could escape. At that exact moment, a small bell chimed, and the captain came over the loudspeaker announcing their arrival at the gate and thanking everyone for flying with them.

"Finally," she whispered under her breath.

Jumping up as quickly as possible, she grabbed her carry on and started to bolt, grateful she was in the first few rows. Escape was in her sights, now if she could only—

"Here," Douchebag held out a small white card. "Call me sometime. I can take you to dinner on my private yacht. Show you what real doctor money is."

She grabbed the card, knowing it was going straight in the first trash can she saw. Was this guy for real? They were in Colorado. No one owned a yacht here. What did he do, take it out on Blue Mesa reservoir and just sit there?

He insults her chosen profession, hits on her, and lies in the process.

What. A. Catch.

Managing a small nod, Josie hurried off the plane, her smile falling as soon as she hit the terminal. After a quick pit-stop to the bathroom—where she ripped up the jerk's card with extreme satisfaction and dropped it in the trash—she made her way to the concord. Now that she had a moment to herself to breathe, her smile returned. The second she hit the terminal she knew her brother Max would be there waiting to pick her up. And then, off to Woodland Hills to start her veterinary internship.

No amount of money could pull her away from her dream job. She'd fantasized of helping animals since she was a kid when she and Max found a bird with a broken wing in their backyard. They'd taken it to the vet where he'd shown them how to care for the sweet magpie. Unfortunately, the poor thing could never fly again, but they found a bird sanctuary where Mr. Featherkins lived out the rest of his days getting the biggest, juiciest worms he could eat.

That moment cemented her life's calling. And her brother's. Considering Max was the vet she was interning with. She couldn't wait to work with her brother. He was the best big brother in the world, even if he did have an annoying habit of leaving the empty milk carton in the fridge.

The underground tram stopped. A robotic voice announced their arrival at the terminal for ground transportation and baggage claim. She was glad Max was picking her up, seeing as how she had to check two very heavy bags. Since she'd stayed in the dorms during school, she didn't have any furniture—thank goodness the place she rented in Woodland Hills came fully furnished—she only had her personal items with her but packing up her entire life and moving across the country wasn't a small task no matter what you had.

Her heart raced as she rode the escalator up to the terminal, excitement causing her to bounce up and down, willing the slow-moving staircase to go faster. She couldn't wait to see Max, couldn't wait to start this new chapter of her life.

Her feet finally reached the top of the escalator. Carefully stepping off, she adjusted the carryon on her shoulder, pushed her glasses up her nose, and stepped out into the large terminal. She scanned the crowd. A few drivers held signs with last names. An older couple stood to the side, holding a stuffed animal, presumably waiting for a visit from a grandkid. A host of people were on their phones, texting, talking, trying to find their loved ones to pick them up.

No Max.

Her heart sank, smile faltering. Where was her brother?

He hadn't forgotten, had he? No. Max wouldn't do that. He specifically asked for her flight number so he could keep track of it. Maybe he was running late? Woodland Hills was a two-and-a-half-hour drive from Denver International Airport. Traffic was always a pain in the city and accidents were common on the mountain roads.

Her heart skipped a beat. Breath freezing in her lungs. Did Max get into an accident? Was he lying on the side of the road after being crushed under a boulder? Did he swerve to avoid a deer, drive off a cliff and—

"Josie!"

At the sound of her name, she turned. It wasn't the deep masculine voice of her brother. But it was familiar. Softer, more feminine. Sexy.

"Bex?"

Josie stared as the dark-haired woman with tattoos covering every inch of her arms started walking her way. What in the world was her brother's best friend doing here?

"I'm here to pick you up," Bex said as if Josie had asked the question out loud.

A mix of shock and nerves hit her stomach. Bex always made her nervous on account of how incredibly hot she found the woman. But then the implication of the situation sunk in, and the fear was back.

Reaching out, she grabbed Bex's arm, unable to keep the worry out of her voice.

"What's wrong? Where's Max? Is he okay? Did something happen—"

"Josie, chill." Bex gently removed Josie's arm, muscles flexing as she crossed her arms over her chest. "Your brother is fine. A mare is foaling. Max had to stay, so he asked me to come get you."

Oh. That made sense. Woodland Hills was ranching country. Her brother specialized in large animals, horses, cows and the like. Usually, the births went fine but having the vet on hand in case of a breech birth was always a good idea.

"You got luggage?"

Knowing her brother was okay, her fear receded, and the spark of excitement came back. Grinning at Bex, she nodded. "Well hello Bex, nice to see you too. The flight? Why yes, it was fine. Had a bit of a chatty Chad as my seatmate, but no turbulence so I call that a win."

Bex stared, not even a hint of a smile. Her brother's BFF wasn't known for her charming wit or small talk. Honestly, it was one of the reasons Josie liked her so much. Bex didn't waste time on insincerity.

But that didn't mean Josie wouldn't take every opportunity she had to have a little fun with the woman.

"Hello Josie. I'm glad your flight was good. Sorry about your seatmate. Do you have any luggage?" Bex replied with a deadpan tone.

"See it's that world class charm that wins people over, Bex."

Bex rolled her eyes, but Josie swore she saw the hint of a smile at the corner of her mouth.

"It's a two-and-a-half-hour drive and getting dark, Saunders."

Translation: stop fucking around and let's go. Seemed like Bex was in a bit of a mood today. Not that she blamed the woman. No one enjoyed having their day interrupted to drive five hours round trip to grab someone.

"Yes, I have luggage. And thank you for picking me up."

Bex shrugged. "Max asked."

Of course. Bex wasn't here for her. She was here because of Max. Josie tried not to let the small sting of disappointment show. Bex and Max were best friends after all. She was just the kid sister. The one who hung around, annoying them, trying to hang out with the older cool kids. No matter that she'd been nursing a huge crush on her brother's BFF for years now. Bex never gave one hint that the attraction went both ways. Didn't matter that she knew Bex was into women, she clearly wasn't into Josie.

They headed to the carousel where her flight's luggage was being dispensed. Her gaze slid to Bex as they stood in silence. Nobody could out silence Bex. The woman was like a statue. Stoic and still. Not her. Josie didn't do well with silence. Another reason she prefered working with animals. They were always chattering, making noises and sounds to fill the silent space. It felt…comforting.

"So how was the drive?"

Bex shrugged. "Fine."

Oh boy, one-word answers. This was going to be a fun trip.

"Any construction on the way?"

Dark brown eyes glanced at her as Bex snorted. "It's Colorado, there's only two seasons, winter and construction."

"Winter and construction," Josie said at the same time.

Bex chuckled, the corner of her mouth curling up. Josie silently cheered at the sight. It wasn't often Bex smiled. She wouldn't even consider this a smile for another person, but for Bex it was a full watt grin. A silent cheer went off inside. She vowed to do whatever she could to see that almost smile as much as possible during the ride.

"Seriously, Josie?"

Bex's question dragged her out of her silent celebration. Josie glanced over to see Bex standing by her two pieces of luggage. She hadn't even seen the other woman pull them off the carousal.

"What?" Josie asked, trying, and failing to hide her grin.

Bex arched one dark eyebrow and looked down at the two large hard-shelled suitcases with a very distinct look.

"Did you just grab those without checking? How do you know they're mine?" She placed her hands on her hips, going for haughty, but clearly failing as Bex gave a dry stare.

"I'm not even dignifying that with an answer."

Okay so her suitcases had a picture of her face on them. Not just her face, but her face giving the goofiest, biggest smile possible. They'd been a gag gift from her former roommate. Allison had them specially printed, claiming no one would walk away with her luggage now. The printing had stretched her face across the hard shell so she looked like a caricature of herself, but to be honest she kind of liked it. It was silly and unique.

Like her.

"Let's go," Bex said, grabbing the handles of both suitcases and heading for the door.

Josie hurried to catch up, reaching to grab one of her bags. "You don't have to—"

"I got it," Bex tugged the luggage closer, refusing to let Josie take one. "Not a problem."

How chivalrous.

Josie sighed. If only Bex was doing it for romantic reasons. Nope. She was on BFF duty. Josie knew Bex would rather be anywhere but here, driving Max's little sister through the mountains at dusk. Oh well, at least she'd get to spend a few hours in the tight confines of a car with the woman she'd been crushing on for over a decade. Absolutely nothing torturous about that.

She was 0 for 2 on seatmates today.

CHAPTER 2

*F*uck! What the hell had she agreed to?

Bex tapped her key fob, the trunk of her sedan opening. How she let Max talk her into driving all the way down to Denver on her day off to grab his sister, she'd never know. No. That was a lie. She knew. Max asked, and she couldn't refuse him. He was her best friend. Through thick and thin. They had always been there for each other. He'd never hesitated to help her out. It really wasn't that big of a deal to drive a few hours and grab Josie.

It was the driving back part she was worried about.

"Still have the Blueberry, nice," Josie said with a smile.

She always smiled. Josie had been wearing that smile ever since Bex met her years ago when she and Max meet in the tenth grade, tried dating and realized they were both gay. The Saunders family had accepted their transition from boyfriend/girlfriend to best friends with ease. Her family... not so much.

"Yup, she's still got life in her," Bex answered, referring to her car she'd named Blueberry after her love of the TV show Psych. It was the first thing she'd bought with her own money. Two summers and every single weekend at the local burger joint in town got her enough cash to buy the used car her senior year. Thanks to diligent maintenance, her sweet Blueberry was still running ten years later.

She started to heft the suitcases into the truck, but Josie placed a soft, warm hand over hers. Bex stilled, the touch sending a wave of feverish need through her. *Dammit!* This was why she hadn't wanted to come pick Josie up. It wasn't that she didn't like Max's little sister. Far from it. The woman was funny and sweet, kind to everyone around her, and fucking beautiful.

That was the problem.

"I can help," Josie said, a big smile lighting up her face. "You don't always have to do everything."

With that, she tossed her blond hair over her shoulder, straightened her glasses, and lifted one suitcase into the trunk with a small grunting sound.

"See," Josie beamed as if she'd just single-handedly won the heavyweight lifting championship.

That smile hit Bex right in the chest, causing a twinge of longing. Brushing the feeling off, she grunted and lifted the other suitcase into the trunk, slamming the lid down.

"This is going to be a very long drive if you stay monosyllabic the whole way," Josie said with a soft sigh.

It was going to be a long ass drive either way. No doubt Josie would talk her ear off. The woman hated silence. Even as a kid she'd been bursting with energy, always filling the quiet spaces with noise. Bex didn't really mind since she never felt she had all that much to say. Plus, Josie had a beautiful voice. Soothing like a warm cup of tea on a rainy day.

Shit!

She needed to stop waxing poetic about her best friend's little sister. Even if it was only in her head. It felt…like a betrayal. Max and his family had been so good to her over the years and here she was, paying him back by perving on his kid sister.

It hadn't always been like this. When Bex first met Josie, she'd been a kid, always tagging along with Bex and Max. Trying to hang with the big kids. Bex hadn't minded. The kid was sweet. Bex hung out at the Saunders' house a lot as a teen, especially after she came out to her parents. They hadn't kicked her out, but they might as well have.

Her mom had sobbed for a solid week after she told them she was a lesbian. Her dad, red-faced and angrier than she'd ever seen him, told her she was a disappointment and the day she turned eighteen, she was on her own.

A threat he made good on.

Thankfully, the Saunders let her crash in their basement on the futon until she'd found a friend to split an apartment with. Max and his family had been her lifesaver. Josie had just been part of the package. Max's little sister.

Much like her older brother, Josie had come out to her family in high school. They all accepted her pansexuality with open arms. The memory still gave Bex conflicted feelings. She'd been happy her friend's family was so loving and supportive, but the pain of her loss, her own family's disownment, still stung. No matter how much time passed.

"Awww, you still have Baby Thor up." Josie tapped the small Thor figurine hanging from the rearview mirror.

"You tied him up there," Bex grunted, clicking her seatbelt into place and jamming the keys into the ignition. "He's impossible to get down."

Two summers ago, on a visit home, Josie won the tiny Thor figurine in one of those quarter machines. She'd then proceeded to tie it to Bex's rearview mirror—since Bex had been the one driving that night—declaring it her good luck charm.

"You're both welders. He's like your patron saint or something, right?"

Bex could have informed Josie that Thor was the god of thunder, not a welder and, seeing as how she wasn't religious, she didn't need a patron saint. But she hadn't had the heart to dim Josie's smile—she may be grumpy, but she wasn't a monster—so she'd shrugged, grunted, and left the damn thing up.

"Admit it," Josie teased. "You like him."

She didn't really have any strong feelings toward the tiny figurine. But she did have some complicated ones toward the woman sitting in the passenger seat next to her.

"Buckle up," she commanded in lieu of an answer.

Josie laughed softly but did as requested.

Bex pulled out of the lot and headed toward the airport exit. She hadn't always felt this off kilter with the woman. For years, Josie had just been another person in Bex's life. A little kid. Max's sister. But the summer Josie came home from undergrad, Bex was hit by a sudden realization. Staring at her, all grown up. Long blond hair cascading around her shoulders. Dark blue frames highlighting her bright hazel eyes. That tiny dimple on her left cheek winking at her from across the room every time she laughed...

Josie was beautiful.

A strange pang of desire hit Bex that night, and she hadn't been able to shake it since. No matter how hard she tried. How many hookups she had. She could not get Josie off her mind. It'd been easier when the other woman had been gone at vet school, states away, the temptation too far to reach. But now...now she was home. Since she planned on joining her brother's veterinarian practice, it looked like she was home for good and Bex was well and truly fucked.

"So, how's things?" Josie asked once they'd paid the parking fee and hit the highway.

"Good."

A heavy sigh sounded from beside her. "Come on, Bex. I know you can speak in complete sentences."

"What?" She glanced over at Josie quickly, frowning, before focusing back on the road again. "Things are good."

"Okay, well, what does "good" mean? The shop going well? Any fun, new commissions?"

Knowing the inquisitive woman wasn't going to let it go, Bex nodded. "Yeah, things are staying steady. Mostly fence repairs and stuff, but I do have a project that's kind of cool. Some LARPing group commissioned me to make a throne for them for an epic battle they have coming up this summer."

"Really? That's so cool!" Josie's voice rose an octave. "I've always wanted to join a Live Action Role Playing group. I played some D&D with my former roommate and her friends in undergrad, but vet school was so time-consuming I had to drop it."

She could just imagine Josie running around the woods in a Wizard's cloak tossing tennis balls at people yelling "firebolt, firebolt, firebolt" and laughing with glee. The image made the corner of her mouth tick up.

"I'm sure interning with Max, I probably won't get much more free time to devote to something as time intensive as LARPing, though." Josie leaned back against her seat, smile slipping.

"I bet your brother would let you take the time off if you really wanted." Max was a great brother.

"Oh no." Josie sat up, turning in her seat to face Bex. "No special treatment because we're related. I already told Max that when I agreed to intern with him."

Bex frowned, following the signs to continue on I-70. "But hasn't the plan always been for you two to work together?"

"Yes, but I don't want him going easy on me just because I'm his sister. I worked my ass off in school, and I don't want anyone thinking I took the easy route working with Max. It just so happens that we both want to work with large animals."

"No one would ever think you don't work hard, Josie. Remember when you organized your parents' thirtieth anniversary party all by yourself?"

Josie waved a hand in the air. "That wasn't a big deal."

"You replicated their first date, down to the same napkins at the pizza restaurant they went to."

A quick glance allowed Bex to see the adorable pink blush staining Josie's pale cheeks.

"I wanted it to be special for them. Max would have helped, but he was in the thick of vet school, and I didn't want to distract him."

"Exactly," Bex pointed out. "Which is why your brother knows how hard you work and won't be opposed to making sure you have time off to do something fun."

"Maybe you could do it with me?"

A rush of heat consumed her at Josie's innocent words. They turned dirty in Bex's mind. The double meaning planting naughty images of her and Josie doing all sorts of things together. Things she was sure Josie's brother would *not* approve of.

Bex cleared her throat, reminding her horny brain they were talking about role playing, and not the naked kind.

"I'm not a big gamer."

"What?" Josie gasped. "You don't want to dress up like a knight and go traipsing through the forest fighting with foam swords? I'm shocked!"

That pulled a half smile out of her. Josie's sassy humor always did. Though she tried to hide it. Tried not to connect with this woman more than they already were. It would only end badly. All of Bex's relationship did. Which was fine. Okay, not fine, but when they ended, at least all that was over was the relationship. If she started anything with Josie and things went south, she'd lose everything.

The Saunders were a tight family. They loved Bex, but Josie was their flesh and blood. If she hooked up with Max's little sister, it'd be a betrayal of their friendship. She'd risk losing the only family she had left, and she would not allow that to happen.

"It's not like my heart is set on LARPing," Josie continued. "It just sounds fun to try one day. But I can wait. Sometimes you have to wait for the things you really want."

Bex glanced over. The way she said that sounded like there was something more to it. What could Josie want? She had her degree, an internship, and then a job with her brother. That's all she'd ever talked about. Maybe it was less of a career want and more of a personal one. Josie could be talking about wanting someone as opposed to something.

The thought made a small prick of green envy slide down her throat. She didn't begrudge Josie her happiness, but hell, if she didn't wish it was possible that Bex could be the one to give it to her.

But it wasn't possible.

She needed to buck up and move on.

And if someone could tell her how the fuck to do that, it'd be great.

Movement caught the side of her eye. She glanced over quickly to see Josie removing the thick blue sweater she'd been wearing, revealing a tight yellow tank top underneath. The thin shirt hugged her breasts, the low scoop of the shirt's cut allowing for a generous portion of cleavage on display.

Bex gripped the steering wheel tighter, clenching her jaw and focusing back on the road. A pulse throbbed between her legs, mouth watering at the sight of all that smooth, creamy skin. It was all she could do not to pull over on the side of the road, toss caution to the wind, and beg Josie to let Bex taste her.

"What are you doing?" she asked instead of doing any of the things she really wanted. Her voice was rougher than she intended, but Josie didn't take offense. Instead, the woman laughed softly, adjusting her glasses as her sweater removal knocked them askew on her face.

"It's warm. I always wear a sweater on planes because they're freezing."

"I could have turned up the air if you wanted."

"No need, I'm fine."

Great. She was fine. Bex wasn't. They had over two hours left on this road trip and literal temptation was sitting right next to her.

CHAPTER 3

"*S*hit!"

Josie shifted her gaze from the window where she'd been watching the trees zoom by. An hour into their journey. Bex had gone silent a while back. Not unusual for Bex, but Josie could swear she felt an odd tension in the air. It was unusual. So strange she did the unthinkable for her. Turned up the music and enjoyed the tunes instead of conversation. She couldn't remember the last time she'd gone this long with someone without talking.

It was oddly nice. Who would have thought?

"What's up?" she asked as she saw Bex's brow furrow.

"We're low on gas." Bex swore. "I should have filled up in the city before we left, but I got distra—"

Bex slammed her mouth shut, cheeks reddening against her freckled cheeks.

"What?"

"Nothing." Bex shook her head. "Never mind. We need to find a place to fill up."

Not many options on the interstate. They were high into the mountain pass, no gas stations, no rest stops, there were barely even any shoulders to pull off on. I-70 was a beautiful drive, but there were remote parts where you were out of luck if you needed something.

Josie pulled out her phone, bringing up her map app. She typed in *gas near me* and hoped the one bar of service she was getting would be enough to find something. Holding her breath, she crossed her fingers as she waited for the spinning dots to reveal their salvation.

"Got it!" She smiled triumphantly and held the phone up. "Take the next exit and there should be a gas station about three miles down."

"Three miles?" Bex groaned. "Why wouldn't they put it right next to the highway?"

She shrugged. "Maybe they didn't have the room or the right zoning."

Josie knew nothing about the laws regarding structures along the highways. But it did seem odd. They usually were right along the main road. Easy for travelers to get gas and get going.

"Maybe it'll be cheaper since it's not right off the highway."

"I wouldn't count on it," Bex grumbled. "I should have gassed up in Denver."

"Oh yes, because the gas prices are so much cheaper in the city."

Bex arched one eyebrow at her sarcastic reply. Josie simply smiled and gave her a wink, which garnered another small smirk from the tattooed badass. She silently cheered. That was two Bex smiles she'd gotten. Would lucky number three be a full reveal? She would bet anything a full Bex smile would knock her on her ass.

"Here's the exit." She pointed to the sign with a small symbol showing gas, food, and lodging on the right side of the road.

"I see it."

Bex slowed the car, guiding it off the highway. After the first mile, the paved road turned into dirt, the car jostling with each and every bump.

"Man, this is out in the sticks," Bex muttered as her hands gripped the wheel after a particularly nasty pothole wrenched the car to the left.

"It does seem a bit out there. Hopefully, this gas station is still in operation." Her maps app wasn't always attuned to the latest closures. A disappointing visit to a closed Starbucks a few weeks ago still stung.

"I swear if we get stuck in the backwoods and run out of gas, I am going to be so pissed," Bex grumbled.

"I'm more worried no one will be there to help." She frowned. "Or someone will be there, but it'll be like a creepy old guy who warns us if 'we go down that way we'll never come back alive.'"

Bex snorted. "You watch too many horror movies."

"They're fun," she insisted. "A safe way to get scared."

"Whatever. If we get murdered by a banjo playing psycho, your brother will never forgive me."

She laughed. "We'll be dead, so I don't think that will matter. Besides, out here I'd be more worried about getting mauled by a bear."

"And now I'm worried too. Thanks, Josie."

She grinned. "That's what I'm here for."

Bex let out a small chuckle. Josie missed this. She'd always enjoyed spending time with Bex. The woman was hilarious. Her humor was a bit on the darker side, but Josie enjoyed it. Bex was the Debbie Downer to her Sally Sunshine. In a weird way, they fit together so well. Now if only she could get Bex to see how well they could fit together in bed, things would be perfect.

She thought she spied a hint of heat in the other woman's

eyes when she stripped off her sweater. Could she have left the sweater on and turned up the AC? Sure. But did she intentionally take it off to showcase what some former partners had called her mesmerizing cleavage? Heck yeah, she had. She'd wanted Bex for far too long, and this drive was the perfect way to see if that desire flowed both ways.

If only the damn stoic woman would loosen up that trademark control a bit. Josie could usually read people pretty well, but Bex held everything so close to the chest. Sometimes she thought she saw the same need reflected in those beautiful dark brown eyes, but then Bex would blink, and it'd be gone. Made Josie wonder if she was just imagining what she wanted to see or if it was real.

"Is that it?" Bex asked, pulling Josie out of her thoughts.

Josie squinted, adjusting her glasses as a building came into view down the road. She glanced down at her phone to see the one bar of service had disappeared. Their little dot on the map was stuck on the highway. She knew refreshing would just give her an error message, so she slipped her phone back into the pocket of her jeans.

"I think so."

As they drove closer, she saw the small building which resembled a log cabin. Out front were two gas pumps. Instead of the normal billboard sign with gas prices listed, there was a small sandwich board sign out front letting cars know they had gas, food, and restrooms for paying customers.

"Looks like it's still up and running."

Bex sighed. "Thank fuck."

They pulled into the parking lot, which even bumpier than the dirt road. The car dipped, sending Josie bouncing in her seat, her head connecting with the roof of the car.

"Ow!"

"Shit!" Bex hit the brakes. "I'm sorry. Are you okay? Fucking road."

"I'm fine," she smiled, rubbing the spot on her head where it connected with the roof.

"Are you sure? Let me see."

Bex grabbed her head, gently tilting it down to inspect her skull. Josie smiled, holding back a soft moan at the feel of Bex's fingers running through her hair. They were warm and gentle as they probed. She hadn't expected gentle. In this position, she had a direct view of Bex's chest. She tried not to be a perv, but her face was literally inches away. Bex's grey v-neck T-shirt gapped a bit, giving her a tiny peek of something black and lacy underneath.

Black lace? On Bex? She was surprised and turned on at the same time.

"I don't see any blood and there's no bump," Bex said. "I think you're okay."

Josie blinked, lifting her head. Her face heated as she tried to erase the image of Bex's bra from her mind. No dice. It was branded there forever. A tempting sight she'd take out on dark, lonely nights.

"Told you I was fine," she said, clearing her throat when her voice came out huskier than she intended.

"Wait, you're all red." The concerned look returned to Bex's face. "Something's wrong."

Yeah, she was turned on because she was a perv who snuck a peek from the woman who was only trying to help her. *Get it together, Josie!* That was not cool, even if it had been an accident. And now Bex sat there looking all concerned that her driving hurt Josie when, in reality, between the touching and inadvertent cleavage peep. She was riding a razor's edge of lust. Her entire body felt hot, her nipples had stiffened, pressing against the thin fabric of her tank top.

How the hell was she supposed to explain that to Bex without sounding like a creeper?

Crossing her arms over her chest, she gave a soft laugh. "I think it's just a blood rush from tilting my head down for too long. It happens sometimes."

It didn't, but it was as good an excuse as any.

Bex gave her a probing look, but then shrugged and turned back to the wheel. Josie let out a sigh of relief. They pulled up to one of the pumps and got out. Bex put her card in the reader, popping the gas tank and fitting the nozzle inside. Josie watched a huge sigh of exhaustion leave the other woman.

"Are you tired?" What a silly question. She drove two and a half hours to get to the airport, and now here she was, driving all the way back. Of course Bex would be tired. Mountain pass driving was no joke.

"I can take over the driving for a bit if you want?" she offered.

A look of pure horror crept onto Bex's face. "Um, no thanks. I got it."

Josie frowned. "It was one time, Bex. One time."

One dark eyebrow rose. "You crashed your brother's car into a ditch, Josie."

"There was a deer!" she protested. "I swerved to miss the deer, and the car got stuck on the side of the road. It wasn't even a full ditch, more like a dip."

Bex chuckled. "Still ran into a ditch."

"I was eighteen. I'm a much better driver now."

"Even so." Bex shook her head. "The answer is no."

Ugh! One mistake years ago and she got branded a terrible driver for life. It wasn't fair. Whatever. If Bex wanted to be stuck with the entire drive herself, that was her choice. Josie would just sit back and relax. No skin off her nose.

"Fine. Then can I at least get us some snacks for the road?

21

Maybe some drinks?"

Bex nodded.

"Yeah, something with caffeine," she said with another wide yawn. "But none of that shitty gas station coffee. Soda or something."

"You got it."

She turned and headed toward the small log cabin with large windows displaying all kinds of road trip style junk food inside.

"Hey!"

At Bex's call, she stopped and turned.

"Good food," Bex insisted, her mouth turning down into a small grimace. "Not that weird shit you and Max like to torture me with on road trips."

A feisty spark lit inside. "Good food," she said with a small nod.

"I mean it, Josie." Bex pointed a warning finger at her. "Don't make me eat trout jerky again. That shit is nasty!"

Actually, it was pretty good, but she and Max loved unique foods and the tiny mountains of Colorado had some of the best odd treats.

"I hear you." She waved as she headed toward the building.

"Yeah, but why do I feel like you're not listening?" Bex called after her.

She was listening. And she was going to get some "good food." The standard chips, donuts, and name brand candy Bex wanted. She was just also going to grab whatever adventurous snack she found, too.

A huge grin curled her lips as she stepped into the gas station building, glancing around at the treasures she'd discovered. Bex needed to loosen up, and Josie was just the person to help her with that.

Time to have a little fun.

CHAPTER 4

*B*ex shoved the gas nozzle back into its base, screwing the cap onto her tank until she heard the clicking noise. As she closed the tank hatch, she flexed her hands, curling them into fists. Her fingers still burned from touching Josie. The soft strands of her honey-colored hair, the warmth of her scalp, imprinted upon her forever.

Fuck!

She shouldn't have touched her. But when the sharp sound of pain escaped her sweet, pink lips, Bex lost all sense. Fear punched her in the gut at the thought that she'd inadvertently hurt Josie. Damn dirt roads. She should have been more careful pulling into the lot. These small town pit-stops never had enough money to do proper maintenance on their roads.

"I shouldn't have touched her," she muttered to her reflection in the car window.

But she had, and now she knew how silky Josie's hair felt. Knew the sweet smell of the honey and coconut shampoo she used. Knew that touching the younger woman sent a crashing wave of pure, red-hot desire rushing through her body.

Max's little sister!

Right, she had to keep reminding herself why giving into these urges was a bad idea. Hell, she didn't even know if Josie would agree to anything if the whole sister thing wasn't an issue. She'd never hit on Bex. Not overtly. Josie was friendly by nature and a lot of people mistook that as flirting. She'd never come right out and told Bex she wanted anything more than friendship.

Not everyone is as direct as you.

She growled at her reflection as the thought filled her mind. True. She had been called direct a lot in her life. And not always positively—just ask any of her ex-girlfriends. Maybe she should ask Josie if she wanted to...

What? Hook up? Date?

Dammit, what the hell was she even thinking? She couldn't have sex with her best friend's little sister. It wasn't even a matter of if Josie wanted to or not. She was off limits. By the rules of friendship and by Bex's own personal rules. She knew anything between them had the possibility of ending badly and, if forced to pick a side, Max would choose his sister. Every time.

Bex wouldn't even blame him. Having a devoted family who stood by you through thick and thin was a gift nobody should waste.

That was it then. She needed to lock up this attraction she had to Josie and move the fuck on.

And no more touching.

Even to check for head wounds.

A bell chimed in the distance. Bex glanced up to see Josie exiting the store, a plastic bag in hand and a huge, mischievous smile on her face. Oh No. That couldn't be good for Bex. Needing a few more minutes of solitude away from the literal personification of temptation, Bex tossed the keys to Josie and headed toward the gas station building.

"I'm going to hit the bathroom before we leave."

Josie nodded.

"Good idea, it's just inside to the left, past the hot dog warmer." She held up the keys, a playful glint in her eyes. "You finally admitting I'm an adult capable of driving?"

Bex held up a finger. "Those are so you can turn the AC on to keep the snacks cool."

She glanced at the bag again. A grimace turned her lips as she tried and failed to see the contents. Damn thing was solid white. Hiding the tortures she knew Josie had in store for her.

"Am I going to be able to eat anything in there, or did you go rogue on me?"

Josie sighed, rolling her eyes. "Yes, Ms. Boring, I got you stuff to eat."

Oh thank g—

"And I got us some fun, new adventures to try."

Josie's eyes lit up. Hard to be mad at someone when they had so much joy on their face, but then Bex remembered the Rocky Mountain Friend Oyster chips Josie and Max had purchased on their road trip a few summers ago. She was still trying to get the taste of fried bull balls out of her mouth to this day.

"I hate adventures."

Josie waved her hand in the air. "Go use the bathroom grumpy pants. I swear it's like you're allergic to fun."

She wasn't allergic to fun, she just preferred eating things that weren't part of an animal's reproductive system.

Josie climbed into the car, sticking to the passenger side as she inserted the key into the ignition and turned it on. Satisfied Josie wasn't going to try to slip into the driver's seat on her, Bex hurried to the small log cabin building. She nodded to the old guy manning the counter. He glanced up from his book to return the nod before ignoring her. After using the facilities and splashing some water on her face, she gave herself another stern pep talk in the bathroom mirror about the appropriate actions one was allowed to participate in with their best friend's younger sibling, and then headed back to the car.

"Here you go," Josie said once Bex slid into the driver's seat and closed the car door. "One ice cold soda brimming with caffeine."

Bex took the drink, being extra careful not to touch the other woman as she handed it over.

"How you can drink that green sludge is beyond me." Josie made a gagging face. "So sugary."

"That's kind of the appeal," she said, twisting off the cap and taking a large swig.

Ahhhh, there was that sugar buzz she needed.

"I'll stick to my fruit juice, thank you very much."

Bex snorted as she put the car in drive and started back on the road. "Are you kidding me? That so-called juice cocktail has just as much sugar as my drink does."

"Does not."

"Check for yourself."

Out of the corner of her eye, Bex noticed Josie shift about as she grabbed both drinks, turning them to read the ingredients on the back.

"Son of a bitch!" Josie swore. "But it's juice! It's supposed to be healthy."

"It's mostly flavoring with, like, a hint of real juice."

"I feel lied to by the snack industry."

"You're a doctor now. Didn't you learn all about nutrition in med school?"

Josie put the drink back in the cup holder and started rummaging through the plastic bag.

"I went to veterinary school. We learned about animal diets."

Bex shrugged. "Humans are animals."

"Oh ha ha, Ms. Literal."

First she was Ms. Boring, now she was Ms. Literal. She was really batting a thousand with the Josie nicknames. Not that she could argue against either. She was who she was.

"Here."

Bex glanced over quickly to see Josie holding a small package out to her. Warily, she leaned back from the offering.

"What is it?"

A small huff puffed out of Josie's lips. "It's chips."

Okay, all well and good, but, "What kind of chips?"

Knowing Josie, they could be anything from banana chips to chocolate-covered pickle chips. The woman loved exploring the weird world of food. It was cute. As long as Bex didn't have to explore it with her.

"Nacho cheese, but I also have Bar-B-Que apple chips in here too if you wanna try something fun."

She quickly grabbed the outstretched bag. "These are fine."

Josie chuckled. "I thought you might say that. They're already open."

"Thanks."

Who would make a Bar-B-Que apple chip? Apples were good. Bar-B-Que was amazing. But the combination sounded atrocious. Why take two delicious things and mash them together to make something disgusting?

The crinkle ripping sound of a bag opening filled the air and the smell of Bar-B-Que invaded her nostril.

"Mmmmm, delicious," Josie said, crunching on a chip.

Bex had to admit, it did smell enticing. Her stomach growled, mouth watering as the tangy Bar-B-Que smell permeated the car. But her brain still screamed at the thought of the combo.

"Sure you don't wanna try?" Josie held up a chip in the air. "Come on, Bex, walk on the wild side for once."

No thank you. The wild side was dangerous. It's how people got broken bones and lost limbs. She'd lost enough in life already. She was happy playing it safe with known quantities. Like nacho cheese chips. But as she crunched down on her safe, cheesy snack, it just didn't satisfy like usual. Something in her called out to take Josie up on her offer. To dare to step outside her comfort zone.

Be a little wild.

"Just one teeny, tiny bite?" Josie persisted.

One bite couldn't hurt, right? And if it was awful, she didn't have to eat anymore. She could try it and see? What was the harm?

"Okay," she finally agreed. "But I'm pulling over in case it's so nasty I have to ralph."

"Fair enough," Josie said with a small laugh.

Bex guided the car over to the shoulder of the road, which was really just a small patch of grass beside the dirt. At least these backwoods roads didn't have a lot of cars to get mad at her for the sudden pull off. Come to think of it, they hadn't seen a single car since they got off the highway.

"Okay," she said, turning in her seat. "I'm ready. Wait!" She grabbed her soda from the drink holder and unscrewed the lid, holding it in her hand like a life preserver.

"Now I'm ready." She nodded, soda chaser in hand.

Josie shook her head, but her smile was wide, enjoying her win in the weird food game.

"Open up," she commanded.

Bex had no idea what possessed her to agree. She was perfectly capable of grabbing her own chip and shoving it in her mouth. But for some reason, she found herself following Josie's order. Her lips parted, and she leaned forward. Josie reached into the bag, pulling out a small roundish shaped chip. Bex could see a hint of the pale, dehydrated apple underneath all the red Bar-B-Que flavoring covering the snack. Her nose wrinkled at the sight.

"Close your eyes," Josie said in a hushed voice.

Bex arched an eyebrow.

"You're letting the visual get to you. Close your eyes so you can experience the flavor without your brain telling you these two things don't go together."

"They don't go together," she insisted.

Josie pursed her lips. Silence filled the car for a few seconds before she said in a serious tone, "Sometimes the things people think can never be good together are the best combinations in the world. They complement each other. Make each other better. You never know unless you try and see."

Bex blinked, wondering if they were still talking about food combinations.

"Close your eyes, Bex."

Without thinking, Bex felt her eyelids fall. Darkness filled her vision. Heightening all her other senses. Josie was right. Now that she couldn't see the apple, the smell of the Bar-B-Que flavoring overwhelmed her, making her salivate.

"Open," Josie commanded.

Bex did as she was told and suddenly, she felt the light pressure of the chip being placed on her tongue. The Bar-B-Que flavoring exploded on her tastebuds. An involuntary moan escaped her as she closed her lips around the tasty treat. But as she did so, she didn't realize Josie hadn't released it yet. Her tongue stroked along Josie's finger and thumb as the woman slowly pulled them from Bex's mouth.

"There," Josie said, brushing her thumb along Bex's lower

lip, catching some flavoring dust stuck there. "That wasn't so bad, was it?"

Bex's eyes snapped open just as Josie stuck her thumb into her own mouth to suck the flavoring off. *Fuck!* She didn't think she'd ever seen anything hotter in her life. And damned if Josie's eyes weren't heavy with desire as she stared at Bex.

Shit! Things just got way more complicated.

CHAPTER 5

*J*osie placed her hand in her lap, squeezing it tight to hide the trembles. Her fingertips still tingled from the feel of Bex's hot, wet tongue. She couldn't believe she did that! It'd been so brazen, so…naughty.

Swallowing down a giggle, she settled back into her seat. A quick glance over to Bex revealed the older woman's muscles tense and flexed as she gripped the steering wheel so hard her knuckles turned white. Josie would be worried she'd gone too far if she didn't see the flush rising up Bex's face. Notice the distinct sharp points of her nipples pressing against her shirt.

She's just as turned on as me.

Celebration bells rang out in her head, but outside she kept it cool. Her little experiment had worked! Bex had shown her hand, and it said the attraction was mutual. Now she just needed a way to broach the subject. Wasn't like she could just blurt out "hey, I see we're both attracted to each other, wanna go on a date? Hit the movies? Skip all that and spend the entire night having hot, sweaty, mind-blowing sex?"

It would be mind-blowing. Of that, Josie was sure. Not to toot her own horn, but she was a generous lover. Many of her former partners had said so. And she'd been hung up on Bex for so long, she couldn't imagine anything but paradise from being with her.

The car bumped and bounced as Bex continued down the road. Silence filled the air. Not unusual around Bex, but this silence felt different. Weighted. There was a ten-ton horny elephant in the car with them, and if Josie didn't talk about it, she knew it would go unmentioned.

"So," she said as casually as she could muster. "I was thinking now that I'm back in town for good, maybe we could—"

"Max said you were renting the other side of the duplex from him," Bex interrupted. "Working together, living next to each other, good thing y'all get along or you'd get pretty sick of each other. The last tenant he had in there was pretty cool. Quiet. Neat. I helped Max clean it out after the guy left so you're move-in ready."

Josie frowned. That was a lot of words in a row for Bex.

"Um, yeah." She frowned, not used to being interrupted by Bex. Bex never interrupted anyone. That would require joining in on a conversation. "He's giving me a great deal, too. I told him I'd pay full price, but you know Max."

"Generous to a fault." Bex nodded. "I mean, he is your brother. Be kind of shitty to charge you full price."

She shrugged. "I don't want special treatment at work because I'm his sister and I don't expect it in my living situation either."

Bex scoffed. "Just be grateful you have a supportive family willing to help you out."

Guilt punched Josie right in the gut. "Bex, I'm sorry, I didn't mean—"

"It's fine." Bex waved a hand in the air, pulling the car back onto the highway on-ramp.

Josie chewed her lip, shame gnawing at her even if Bex seemed unfazed. She hadn't meant to sound ungrateful. She loved her brother and appreciated everything he and their parents had done over the years to help her. As much as she wanted to prove she could succeed on her own, having a family to fall back on was a privilege she shouldn't take for granted. Not when she knew the alternative.

Josie had been there when Bex came out to her parents. Not in the actual room, but she was around for the aftermath. She saw how much it destroyed Bex when her parents rejected her. The pain radiated off her for years. Still did. Josie knew Bex hadn't spoken to her parents since they kicked her out of the house on her eighteenth birthday.

Talk about the shittiest birther present ever.

No.

The shittiest parents ever!

She'd wanted to run over to the Kirkel house and scream at Bex's parents. But she'd been just a teenager herself. Now here she was, being a brat about taking help from her family when Bex had lost hers just for being herself.

Mood sufficiently killed, Josie bit back another apology she knew Bex wouldn't take and changed the subject.

"Hey, how's Crusher?"

The corner of Bex's mouth kicked up in a small smile.

That's another one! Josie smiled gleefully.

"He's good," she answered with a small chuckle. "Got him a new tank just last week, and he's been preening under the sunlamp like a prima-donna."

Crusher was Bex's tortoise. She found him on the side of

the road, missing a leg from an animal attack. Luckily, Max had been able to nurse the poor guy back to health. Best guess was, he was somebody's pet. They got tired of taking care of him and let him loose in the wild, thinking he'd be okay. Max had been livid, Josie and Bex too. Domesticated pets couldn't live in the wild, which was probably how Crusher got injured.

No one knew how old he was—it was almost impossible to tell a tortoise's age without record keeping—but since they could live upwards of one-hundred years, Josie would guess the sweet guy might even outlive Bex. He was the perfect pet for the woman sitting next to her. A hard outside shell, but soft and warm on the inside. The analogy was almost too perfect.

"I'm excited to have a place to settle down so I can finally get a pet."

Living in school housing for the past eight years had been fine, but she hadn't been allowed to have any pets. As an animal lover, that really stunk. The first thing she was doing once she got all settled was adopting a critter in need from the shelter. After all, what kind of vet didn't have an animal of their own?

"What are you thinking of getting?" Bex asked.

"Whatever animal needs me the most."

A soft chuckle came from the driver's side. "Yup, sounds about right."

A soft rumble sounded in the distance. Josie glanced out the car window, but the sun had started setting behind the mountains. The dark clouds in the sky could be a signal of an impending storm or just twilight setting in.

"Was that thunder?" she asked.

"Shouldn't be." Bex frowned. "I didn't see any chance of rain predicted today."

Yeah, but this was Colorado. If they said it was going to pour, they got a few sprinkles, and a clear sky meant flash flooding. You could never trust the weather predictions out here.

Josie pulled out her cell and clicked on her weather app, but of course, she had no service yet again. Damn mountain pass. The reception was so spotty.

"We're only about an hour and fifteen from home," Bex said, eyes scanning the sky before turning back to the road. "Hopefully it holds off until then."

Hopefully, but she wasn't counting on it. She crossed her fingers and ankles, willing the weather to hold off. Driving the twisty mountain highway in the rain was a nightmare. Even worse than in the snow because at least when it was snowy, people tended to slow down. Rain didn't faze drivers. They still zoomed by at unsafe speeds. She hated it.

Suddenly, she was very glad Bex hadn't agreed to let her drive.

"You going to be okay? Driving in the rain?"

Bex gave her a dry look out of the corner of her eyes. "I'll be fine. I'm not the one that drove off the road, remember?"

"One time. One time!" Could no one let that go?

She sunk back against her seat, crossing her arms over her chest.

"And like I told you, I swerved to miss a deer. Hitting it would have caused significant damage to the car."

And her too. Hitting a deer had been known to kill people. Plus, the thought of hurting any animal, even unintentionally, ripped her heart out. The one time in school she had to assist in putting a dog down, she'd cried for a week. Even knowing they were helping the sick old animal find peace, it still cut her to her core.

"I'm not saying it wasn't the right thing to do," Bex agreed. "But I am saying it'll be a cold day in hell before I let you drive the blueberry."

"According to some mythology, hell is frozen over in ice,

so I guess hand the keys over."

"Nice try."

She shrugged. "Worth a shot."

They drove on in silence for a bit, the distant sounds of rumbling thunder getting closer, the threatening sound driving up Josie's worry. To distract herself, she did what she always did. Talked.

"So do you let anyone drive your car?" she asked Bex. "Max? Your girlfriends?"

Bex snorted. "No. Your brother has his own car and the last girlfriend I had was two years ago. Also not allowed to drive the Blueberry."

Two years ago? Interesting. She wondered why such a long dry spell. Or maybe not a dry spell. Just because Bex wasn't dating anyone didn't mean she wasn't hooking up with anyone. Josie frowned. She didn't like thinking about Bex with anyone. Not that she begrudged the woman her happiness. She just...wanted to be the one providing that happiness.

"No girlfriend, huh?"

"Nope."

"Hooking up with anyone?"

Bex quickly glanced over at her, brow furrowed. "Why are you so interested in my sex life, Josie?"

Because I want to be a part of it.

Probably shouldn't say that. Instead, she shrugged and smiled, letting Bex come to her own conclusion.

Bex turned her focus back to the road and sighed. "Look, I think we need to talk about—"

Whatever she was about to say was interrupted by a loud popping sound.

"Shit!"

Bex gripped the wheel tight as the car started to shudder and shake. Josie's hand flew out, grabbing the door handle, bracing herself back against the seat as an ominous hissing sound filled the air.

"Hold on!" Bex shouted.

Josie squeezed her eyes shut, praying to the universe that the car didn't careen off the side of the mountain. A stream of colorful four-letter words sailed out of Bex's mouth, filling the car with their creativity.

"I'm taking this exit!"

At Bex's yell, she opened her eyes to see an off ramp. A small one, with nothing but a sign indicating lodging and gas a mile down the road. She would have preferred one of the exits with the gas stations right off the ramp, but emergency situations didn't exactly cater to desires.

They pulled off the highway, the car jerking under Bex's firm grip. A loud boom sounded in the distance, causing Josie to let out a small squeak of surprise.

"Josie?"

Bex's attention wavered for a split second at her cry, long enough to have the car lurching to the right.

"Bex, look out!" She screamed as the headlights illuminated a metal traffic barrier at the end of the ramp they were headed right for.

"Shit!" Bex turned the wheel hard. Too hard.

A horrible sound like metal on pavement screech as the car sailed across the road. Bex tried to over-correct, but whatever happened to the car to set them on this path was clearly making it hard for the woman to control it. They jostled and skidded along the road. Dirt flew up in the air around them as the pavement disappeared. Another loud pop and hiss filled the air, causing the car to jerk uncontrollably. The front tires hit a nasty dip, and she grabbed the 'oh-shit' handle above her head, holding back another scream as the car slid to the side of the road and landed directly in the ditch.

CHAPTER 6

$\mathcal{B}$ex let out another string of curses as the car came to a jarring stop. Heavy breathing filled the air as silence fell. Her hands ached from the tight grip she had on the steering wheel. Every muscle pulled tight, ready to snap.

Fuck!

A small whimper from the side caught her attention. She glanced over to see Josie, wide-eyed and trembling, a hand covering her mouth. Cold, sharp fear filled her at the sight. She turned in her seat, swearing when her seatbelt pulled tight against her chest, pulling her back. Quickly, she released the buckle and shifted forward in her seat. Her hands gently grabbed Josie's shoulders, stroking softly, trying to comfort and at the same time check for injuries.

"Shit, Josie, I'm so sorry. Are you okay? Did you hurt anything?"

Josie's head shook back and forth and that's when Bex realized the woman wasn't holding back tears...she was holding back laughter.

"Josie?"

A strange reaction to have after an accident, but people

reacted to intense situations in all kinds of ways. While she'd hate to see Josie break down crying, Bex wasn't sure laughter made her feel any better. Hysterical laughter usually came right before hysterical crying.

"What—what was—" stifled laughter broke up her words.

Bex raised one eyebrow, not sure if she should be worried or insulted that the other woman found this situation so funny.

"What was that you said about me driving into a ditch?" Josie finally managed to get out before bursting into laughter.

Bex grumbled, sitting back in her seat.

"I'm sorry, Bex, but this is hilarious!"

Really? She didn't sound sorry, and Bex didn't find it all that funny. Her car was in a ditch and judging by what happened on the highway, probably had a flat.

"Oh, come on," Josie said, when she still didn't crack a smile. "You have to admit, it's a little ironic. You refused to let me drive because I drove into a ditch, and then what happens? You drive into a ditch!"

"That's not ironic, it's coincidental."

Josie shrugged. "It's situational irony."

"It's a pain in my ass, is what it is," she grumbled. "Stay here."

Opening the car door, she stepped outside, slamming the door with a bit more force than necessary. She wasn't mad at Josie. Truth be told, it was kind of a funny happenstance. Would have been a lot funnier if it hadn't happened to her.

It did put a kink in their plans to get back home in the next hour. Bex was pretty sure the popping sound she heard was a flat tire. Luckily, she had a spare in the trunk. She'd changed many a flat in her day. Wouldn't take more than half an hour tops then they'd be back on the road.

She made her way around the car, ignoring the rumbling

of the storm the meteorologist promised wasn't coming. All she had to do was change this flat before the rain started and—

"Shit!" she swore as she glanced at the back of the car.

"What's wrong? Flat tire?"

She whirled around to see Josie a few feet behind her. She hadn't even heard the woman get out of the car.

"I thought I told you to stay."

Light brows furrowed, hazel eyes narrowing as Josie glared at her. "I'm not a dog. I just take care of them."

Right, she supposed her command had been a tad rude, but she hadn't wanted Josie out in the dark in the middle of bum-fuck nowhere. There might not be any cars or people around, but it was past dusk now. Prime hunting time for a lot of the forest animals. And Bex did not intend to have herself or Josie on the menu.

"Sorry," she apologized, turning back to the car. "Yeah, it's a flat. Two flats, actually."

"Well...shit indeed."

Yup. One flat they could deal with, but two? She didn't have two spare tires. No one did. How the hell did her car get two flats at the same time? She was diligent about car maintenance. Her tires were only a few years old. They still had hundreds of miles left on them. Did she run over something?

"Should we call a tow truck?" Josie asked. "Do you have roadside service?"

Roadside service in Woodland Hills? The town had one auto body shop. One tow truck. And zero roadside service plans. Since she barely left the small town, she'd never invested in any kind of nationwide one.

"Yes, and no."

Josie rubbed her arms, glancing around their dark forest surroundings. The temperature had dropped with the sun. It was still fairly warm, but after the scare they just had, it was no wonder the younger woman would be cold. Bex opened the back door, reaching into the backseat. Her hand hesitated over the sweater Josie had stripped off earlier and tossed back there. She should grab it. It was Josie's, after all. But something within Bex compelled her to skip the sweater and instead grab her own discarded flannel she'd placed there earlier today. Pulling the soft garment out, she stood and handed it over.

"Here," she said, holding the shirt outstretched toward Josie. "Put this on."

Josie accepted the flannel with a smile, slipping her arms into it and pulling it tight. A powerful, warm sensation hit her low in the gut. Seeing Josie wear something of her's…Bex liked it.

Too much.

Josie maintained eye contact as she brought the collar of the shirt up to her face and inhaled. A small moan of pleasure had her eyes closing and Bex thought she might damn near lose it at the sensual sound. Fuck! Maybe giving Josie her shirt had been a bad idea.

"Thank you," Josie said softly.

Bex nodded, turning back to the flat tires to try and compose herself. She was playing with fire, and she didn't even know why she was doing it. Chalk it up to the shock of the accident. She'd lost her head for a moment. But now she needed to get shit together. They had two flat tires and a storm approaching. She needed to stop walking the line with this Josie temptation and get it together.

"I'm going to look up a local tow and call them," she said, pulling out her phone.

"No, you're not."

She turned her head at Josie's confident words. The blonde held up her hand, cell phone clutched tight, and shook her head.

"No service."

Bex glanced down at her phone and swore. "Dammit! Are you freaking kidding me!"

Stranded on the side of the road, two flat tires, not a car in sight, and a storm headed their way. Could things get any worse?

Don't you fucking dare say that!

She admonished her own thought, knowing that was the exact way to tempt fate to do worse. Instead, she tried to think of a plan.

"Okay, I'm going to head up to the highway and flag down a car. Hopefully, someone can drive me to the nearest town, and I can get some help." She nodded to Josie. "You stay in the car and wait for me. Lock the doors and don't open them until I get back."

Josie shook her head. "That's a terrible idea."

It wasn't great, but at least it was a plan.

"It's too dark for you to stand on the side of the highway," Josie said with a small frown. "Without the car hazards blinking, no one will be able to see you until it's too late."

She had a point, but Bex didn't have any other ideas. She couldn't magically fix the tires or create cell service to call for help. And she sure as hell wasn't counting on any cars coming along this dirt road anytime soon. This exit was barely marked. It wasn't a highly trafficked area.

"Then what do you suggest we do?"

Josie bit her lip, glancing around as if an answer would suddenly pop out of the forest and save them. Ha! The only thing popping out of that forest was a bear. And saving wouldn't be top on its list of things to do to them.

"I saw a picture on the exit sign for lodging and gas a mile down the road." Josie pointed down the dark dirt road. "We could head that way and check it out. They must have a land-line we can use to call for help."

Worth a shot. Better than staying here and hoping someone came along.

She nodded. "Yeah, okay. Let's do it."

Josie smiled, the sight so beautiful it sucked Bex's breath away. Damn, the woman had a glorious smile. It brightened up any situation. Even one as shitty as this.

"Need to grab anything from the car before we go?"

Bex popped the trunk and grabbed the emergency backpack she kept in there with water, a snack, a book, and a change of clothes. She had no idea how long this might take. Better to be prepared for a couple hours' wait.

"I should grab my purse," Josie said, coming around to the trunk. "It's in my carryon."

Bex grabbed the small bag, handing it over so Josie could get her purse out, but she simply slung it over her shoulder after taking it from Bex's hand.

"Actually, I might as well just take the whole thing. I can stuff the rest of the snacks in it in case we get hungry waiting."

Looked like they were both on the same page. That was good. Bex was grateful Josie didn't seem to be upset by this setback. She knew the younger woman had always been very go with the flow type attitude, but this flow was seriously fucked up. It would mess with even the calmest person's cool.

Bex shut the trunk, locking the car after Josie secured the snacks in her carry on.

"Sorry about all this." She waved at her broken car. "Not exactly the welcome home you were expecting, huh?"

"Bex," Josie frowned, coming to her side and placing a hand on her cheek.

Bex froze. Every nerve ending in her body acutely attuned to Josie's touch. Her heart raced at the feel of the woman's smooth palm against her cheek. Her blood boiled, body heating as she stared past the glass lenses into the most beautiful pair of hazel eyes she'd ever seen. Eyes that haunted her dreams with whispers of promises she could never have.

"This wasn't your fault." Josie whispered. "You weren't even supposed to be here. You were helping, like you always do, because you're a good person."

She wouldn't go that far. Sure she'd help out Max. He was her best friend. Wasn't like she was offering to do favors every day for strangers. The way Josie was talking made Bex sound like a saint or something.

"I appreciate the pick up," Josie continued. "And the rest is just a fun little adventure we get to laugh about for years to come."

"You have a strange sense of adventure, Josie."

Josie ginned, leaning in and placing a soft kiss on Bex's cheek. Shock held her immobile. Josie pulled away and started down the road. It took Bex a moment to return to herself. The kiss had been so...unexpected. It wasn't big. Just a soft brush of her lips against Bex's skin. But the fire it lit within had started to rage out of control.

"What the hell was that for?"

Josie glanced over her shoulder with a heavy sigh. Okay, yeah, maybe her question had come out a little harsher than intended, but Bex was so confused right now. If she didn't know any better, she'd say Josie was throwing her the signal. But that was ridiculous. She was Max's little sister. She wasn't interested in Bex...was she?

"It was to thank you for coming out to get me. Now hurry up slowpoke. We need to get going before the storm—"

But whatever Josie was about to say next was drowned out by a loud crack of thunder, followed by the pounding sound of rain as the skies opened and drenched them.

CHAPTER 7

*J*osie stepped into the small office of the roadside motel, rivulets of water pouring off her, gathering in a puddle at her feet. She let out a small sigh of relief at the warmth of the building. The rain had soaked them. Not a gentle light smattering, but a full-on downpour. They'd run the entire mile until they saw the lights of the motel. Her hair was drenched, hanging around her face like wet, stringy noodles. Her cheeks stung from the cold, icy pellets of rain.

Thankfully, Bex's flannel had kept her arms and chest warm, but the thing was soaked, and now that she was inside, she could feel the water seeping past the cloth to her skin. But the worst was her socks. Soaked and squishy in her sneakers. Ew! Nothing was worse than wet socks.

"Oh my! Will you look at you two. Come in. Come in. Get out of that storm."

Josie lifted her head at the gentle voice to see a small woman with light brown complexion. Small wrinkles graced the corners of her eyes and mouth. She stood behind an oak desk, computer in front of her, a worried smile on her face.

"Thank you." Josie smiled back, wincing as her shoes made another squishing sound when she took a step. "Sorry about the mess."

"Think nothing of it, sweetheart." The woman dipped down behind the desk. Reemerging with two white, fluffy towels. She rounded the counter and handed one to Josie and the other to Bex. "I get truckers in here day and night covered in dirt and mud, and who knows what else. We don't mind a little mess at the Hideaway Motel. That's why we have hot showers in every room. Best water pressure on I-70."

The woman beamed.

Josie rubbed the towel against her hair, squeezing the strands to soak up the rain. She wasn't sure "best water pressure" was a selling point for most people, but a hot shower sounded like heaven right now.

"We don't need a room," Bex said, rubbing the towel along her bare arms. "Our car got a flat. Two, actually. We were just hoping we could use your phone to call a tow?"

"Of course, dear." The woman shuffled back behind the counter, turning the desk phone toward Bex. "You want to call Sonny's towing, the number is right here, you tell him Mabel sent you."

"Thank you," Bex said, grabbing the small card Mabel held in her hand.

As Bex called the tow truck, Josie glanced around the room. It was clean, sparse. Looked like any other roadside motel office. A picture of a duck flying over a lake with mountains in the back hung on one wall. Two chairs and a small table were set up in the corner next to a sideboard that had one of those coffee pod machines.

"Would you like something warm to drink?" Mabel offered, nodding toward the machine. "Might be a bit late for coffee, but I have some nice herbal tea over there. Have something while you wait. It'll warm you up."

Josie smiled, heading over to the machine. "Thank you."

The motel might be like any other, but the hospitality was off the charts. Maybe it was because they both looked like drowned rats, or maybe Mabel was just this friendly. Whatever the reason, Josie was glad that if they had to be stranded for a few hours, it was somewhere warm and comforting.

"Damn." Bex's soft curse floated on the air in the quiet room. "No, no, I understand."

Josie set about making some tea. Popping the pod in the machine and pressing the handle down. All the while keeping half her focus on Bex and the frustrated expression on her face. That couldn't be good.

Another crack of thunder caused her to jump, a tiny squeak of surprise escaping her. The lights flickered, but stayed on.

"Don't worry," Mabel said from the desk. "That storm might be bad, but we have a backup generator in case the power fails. The lights will stay on while you wait for Sonny."

She smiled at the woman, pulling the finished tea out and making another cup.

"We'll be waiting a while," Bex sighed, hanging up the phone. "Guess we're going to need that room after all, Mabel."

"What?" Josie rushed over to Bex's side, holding out the steaming drink. "He can't come out to fix the car?"

Bex accepted the drink with a small nod of appreciation, then shook her head. "Nope. Flash flood warning. Roads aren't safe to travel."

"Shoot!" On the bright side, it might have been a good thing they got the flats and had to pull off the highway. Being on the interstate with flash flood rain was not only terrifying, it was dangerous.

"He said he'd come out first thing in the morning."

"Well," Mabel said, shifting behind her computer screen. "Let's get you two a room then."

Josie hoisted her bag onto her shoulder, grateful she'd had the foresight to bring the carry on as it had her bathroom supplies and a change of clothes. As Mabel typed away on the computer, she hurried back to the pod machine and grabbed her tea. When she came back to the desk, Mabel was sliding two key cards into a paper envelope.

"A break in your bad luck, ladies. We have a room available."

A room? As in one? A smile curved her lips. Maybe this disaster could prove to be a blessing in disguise. Her very own romcom moment. Two people with clear sexual chemistry stranded for the night in a motel room…with only one bed. It was a sign from the universe.

"Thank you," Bex said, pulling her wallet from her pocket. "We'll take it."

"I've got this," Josie said, placing her tea on the counter and pulling her purse from her carry on. She whipped out her credit card and handed it over to Mabel.

"Josie, you don't have to—"

"I insist." She smiled at Bex. "You drove, so consider this my gas contribution."

Bex huffed out a small laugh. "I know gas is expensive, but not that expensive."

"You also have two tires to patch, or possibly replace," she pointed out.

Bex grimaced. "Good point, okay you can pay."

Josie beamed, happy with her win. She thought she heard a small chuckle from Mabel as the woman processed her card.

"Okay, you two are all set." Mabel slid the paper envelope holding the keys across the counter, handing Josie back her credit card. "Room 103. Go out this side door and stay under the awning to avoid the rain. Third door down. Can't miss it."

"Thank you, Mabel." She smiled as she grabbed the envelope, putting her card away before grabbing her tea.

Bex held the door open for her. Josie gave her a grateful smile as she slid past back out into the storm. The rain hadn't let up even a bit. Flashes of lightning lit the sky as the deep rumbles of thunder followed. Josie tugged the towel Mabel had given her tighter around her shoulder and rushed along the small awning covered sidewalk toward their room. Small pricks of raindrops hit her face as the wind threw them sideways, but they were mostly protected as they made it to door 103.

She pulled out a keycard and slid it into the lock. The tiny light on top blinked green. Josie turned the knob and pushed open the door to reveal…

Two beds.

Seriously?

Could the universe not give her one damn romcom moment?

"Something wrong?" Bex asked as she shut the door behind them. "Sorry, silly question. Everything is wrong."

No. Not everything. Just her hopes and dreams of cuddling in bed with the sexy woman next to her. Josie turned to see a dark frown on Bex's face, but there was more emotion underneath.

Failure.

"Hey," she said, gently placing her hand on Bex's arm. "Everything is fine. We had a little setback, but we're safe, warm, and we have a place to sleep."

Two places, unfortunately.

"You should call Max, let him know what happened."

Translation, she thought she failed Max in bringing his

sister home and now was too ashamed to call her own best friend. Josie sighed, wishing Bex could see herself through Josie's eyes. See what an amazing and wonderful person she was. Accidents happened, none of this was Bex's fault.

Josie checked her cell, still no service. Glancing around the room, she saw a landline on the small table between the two beds. Grabbing the receiver, she dialed nine, then brought up her brother's number in her contacts, grateful her phone still had battery life. She really should start memorizing cell numbers.

He picked up on the first ring.

"Hey Jojo, you two almost here? This storm is getting pretty nasty."

"Hey Max-A-Million." The sound of her brother's voice soothed some of her ragged nerves. "No, we had a bit of a setback. Won't make it home tonight."

"Why? What happened?" Her brother's voice lost all its jovial tone, worry filling his words.

She explained about the flat tires, pulling off the road, running through the storm, and landing at the motel.

"So we're gonna stay here tonight until the tow guy can come out tomorrow morning. Hopefully, the tires just need a patch and not a replacement."

"Damn, that's bad luck, but I'm glad y'all are safe. How's Bex?"

Grumpy as ever.

Josie glanced over her shoulder to see Bex rummaging through her bag, a scowl on her face.

"She's fine."

Her brother chuckled. "Yeah, sure she is. Blaming herself for an accident and forces of nature?"

She laughed along with him. "Yup."

"That's Bex," he sighed. "Try to convince her this wasn't her fault."

"I'll try, but you know Bex."

At the sound of her name, the woman glanced up and glared at Josie. She smiled brightly, pulling the headset away as she directed her next words to Bex.

"Max says it's not your fault. He's glad you're here keeping me safe. You're doing an excellent job, and you're his hero."

Bex snorted. "He didn't say that."

"I appreciate you, Bex," her brother's voice called out loudly over the phone.

Bex scoffed again, but her lips did curl up into a small smile.

"We both do," Josie said before putting the phone back to her ear and continuing the conversation with her brother.

After they were done talking, she hung up the phone and headed toward the bathroom. A nice, warm shower sounded like heaven right about now. Her feet were all cold and pruny in her shoes. Tiny little wrinkled icicles.

"I'm going to take a shower," she said.

Bex nodded. "I'll go after you."

Josie paused at the bathroom door. This day had not gone as she planned. She thought she'd be getting a few hours in the car with her brother before settling into her new home, but instead she'd gotten a wild road trip with the woman she'd been crushing on for years. Complete with a near death experience, run through the rain, and an overnight stay together. Even if they did have two beds instead of one, they were still in a forced proximity type situation.

Another romcom classic.

Plus, there were those few moments over the past two hours. The touches, the heated looks, the…connections. There was something here. Something between them. If she didn't acknowledge it now, then when? It felt like the perfect time. A sign from the universe.

Gathering up all her bravery, Josie leaned against the open bathroom door frame, staring at Bex, allowing all the desire and emotion she felt for this woman to show in her eyes.

"You could join me," she offered softly. "In the shower. We could…conserve water."

Bex's eyes grew wide as she stared back, shock and hesitation filling them, but also a hint of need. Want. Josie latched onto those last few and hung on with everything she had.

"I want you, Bex," she whispered into the stillness of the room. "Have for a while and I think…I think you want me too?"

She hadn't meant it to sound like a question, but her confidence was running out. As much as she thought she'd seen the heat in Bex's eyes, she couldn't be one-hundred percent sure. She desperately craved confirmation from the woman herself.

"I…"

Josie held her breath, watching as Bex struggled to find the words.

"I…you're Max's sister," Bex finally said, casting her eyes to the ground.

She wanted to scream, yell, throw something against the wall in frustration. Instead, Josie remained calm, keeping her voice as steady as possible. "No. I'm my own person. Just because my brother is your best friend doesn't mean we can't be together. We're both adults. What we consent to do together has nothing to do with anyone else."

Bex glanced back up, hope and desire burning in those beautiful brown eyes. Josie smiled, heart racing at the sight. She was sure this was it. The moment she'd been waiting years for. She was finally going to get to be with—

"I can't," Bex said softly, deflating, her eyes losing their spark as she turned to face one of the beds.

A sharp pain sliced through her. Josie sighed, rubbing at her chest. Rejection never felt good, but this was more. This was a dream she'd held onto for years. Washed away as easily as the rain erased their footprints in the dirt. Hoping this wasn't the end, she nodded and headed into the bathroom.

"If you change your mind," she called over her shoulder. "I'm right here."

She closed the door softly, but left it unlocked, hoping she'd soon be joined in the shower.

I'm right here.

And she always would be, for Bex, she always would be.

CHAPTER 8

*B*ex didn't follow Josie into the shower.

She couldn't. Honestly, she'd been so shocked by Josie's proposal she hadn't known what to say or do.

I want you, Bex.

The words still rang in her ear. Tempting her, tormenting her. Josie wanted her. Her! Little Ms. Sunshine, who could have her pick of any person in the world, wanted tattooed, grumpy, Bex.

Why?

She still couldn't wrap her head around it. Bex had met some of Josie's former dates and they ran the gamut of genders and personalities. She knew the woman didn't discriminate or have a type, but she never imagined any real possibility of Josie wanting her.

But she does.

And she was still Max's sister.

A fact Bex couldn't move past.

She was still arguing with herself when the water in the bathroom shut off. Still sitting on the far bed when Josie came out in a pair of shorts and a thin tank top. The usually sunny woman had a slight frown on her face. Guilt pooled low in Bex's stomach, knowing she put it there. No one liked to be rejected. But she just couldn't justify hooking up with Josie. She was younger than Bex, only by a few years, but it was enough that she might only be looking for a hookup.

She knew one night with Josie would never be enough, but she also knew more than one night wasn't possible. The longer they were together, the more potential for them to break up, which would lead to hurt feelings and side choosing. As she'd gone over in her head before, her side would not be the winning one. She couldn't risk losing Max and his parents if things went south. Hell, she couldn't risk losing Josie in her life either. Right now, it was safe. Josie was her best friend's sister. A fixture in Bex's life. She didn't want to risk the possibility of losing that. Losing her.

"Bathroom's all yours," Josie said, her voice missing that happy spark.

Bex muttered a thank you, grabbing her bag and heading toward the bathroom. After a lukewarm shower—because she didn't deserve a hot one—she brushed her teeth and changed into the long sleep shirt she kept in her go bag.

By the time she opened the bathroom door, the room was dark. Bex turned the bathroom light off, the only illumination coming from the small night light strip under the bathroom mirror. She made her way to the far bed, depositing her backpack on the floor. A quick glance over revealed a curled-up lump in the other bed.

"Goodnight, Josie." She muttered, slipping under her blankets.

"Would be a better night if…" The rest of the words were mumbled softly.

Bex's guilt twisted into a sense of irritation. Didn't she see Bex was doing this for her own good? For their own good? They couldn't hook up and pretend everything was fine in the morning. Max asked her to pick up Josie because he trusted her to take care of his little sister. What kind of best friend would she be if she took that trust and twisted it by bedding the woman?

She should go to sleep. Let it lie. But today had been a shittastic pain in her ass. One issue after another and sleep was the farthest thing from her mind.

"You got something to say, Jojo, say it."

"Don't call me that!" Josie growled. "Only Max calls me that."

Exactly. Which was why Bex said it. She was trying to remind herself why Josie was off limits.

"What's got your panties in a twist?" Why she kept pushing, she didn't know, but Bex couldn't stop herself.

Josie rolled over, clicking on the bedside lamp and glaring. "Not you, that's for sure."

"The fuck does that mean?"

"Ugh!" She let out a half-growl, half-scream sound. "I mean, I'm pissed off because I'm horny and can't do anything about it since we're in a tiny motel room and the woman I propositioned turned me down flat. So please go to sleep and let me wallow in my embarrassment without commentary. Thank you very much."

Bex didn't even know where to begin with that statement. Her brain had short-circuited when Josie said she was horny. Such a dirty word coming from such sweet lips. Heat burned her from the inside out.

"I get that you don't want me. I'm embarrassed I asked, so let's just forget it."

"You think I don't want you?" The words were out before Bex could stop them.

Josie paused, her scowl disappearing as her eyebrows climbed her forehead. "Well…yeah. Why else would you—"

"Because you're Max's sister. Don't fuck the sibling. It's in the best friend code, I'm pretty sure."

White teeth came out to nibble on her full lower lip. "So... if I wasn't Max's sister?"

Bex frowned. "Why ever torture ourselves with a question like that?"

"Torture?" Josie's frown came back. She tossed back her cover, scooting to the edge of her bed. "Bex, do you want me?"

Realizing she'd just revealed her hand, Bex shifted in the bed, turning away from Josie, and plopping down on her pillow.

"That's not relevant. Go to sleep, Josie."

"It's pretty fucking relevant to me."

Hearing a curse come out of her mouth, Bex rolled over, tossing the covers off and standing. She couldn't handle this shit anymore. She was so frustrated and turned on and tired of holding back. Everything was coming to a boiling point, and she felt like she was going to explode.

"Yes, okay! Yes, I fucking want you, Josie. I want to tear off that tank top and those sexy little sleep shorts and taste every inch of you. I want to drive you to the brink of control, then push you over the edge. I want to hear you scream out my name as I taste your release on my tongue. I want to give you so much pleasure you can't stand straight for the next week, okay? Are you happy now?"

Josie stared wide-eyed, slack jawed. Bex swallowed hard, fearing she'd revealed too much, said something wrong. But then, Josie stood, coming closer until they stood a hairbreadth apart.

"I want that too, with you," she whispered.

Her hand reached out, gently resting on Bex's stomach. The heat of Josie's palm seared her through the thin fabric of her sleep shirt. It was all too much. Too intense. Too hard to resist. She couldn't do it anymore.

"Fuck it," she growled, grasping Josie's hips to pull her closer. Bex's mouth slammed down on Josie's, their lips clashing in a wild, unbridled kiss. A soft, squeaky moan escaped Josie, fueling Bex on. She deepened this kiss, tangling her tongue with Josie's drinking in her taste until she was drunk with the sweetness.

Her hands gripped the thin tank top, tugging it up. Josie pulled back, lifting her arms as Bex stripped the tank top from her and threw it across the room. A soft curse left her as she gazed at what she'd revealed. Josie's breasts were perfect. Dusky pink nipples stood erect and begging for attention. Bex's mouth watered as she stared, unable to resist their call.

She dipped her head, taking one turgid peak between her lips. Josie cried out, hands tangling in Bex's hair, pulling her head closer. She chuckled.

"Like that?" she asked before gently biting down.

"Yes, more," Josie panted.

Bex obliged, torturing one sweet nipple before moving on to the other.

"Bex...I need..."

Bex lifted her head, reveling in the warm pink flush running up Josie's chest. She put that there. It took everything in her not to howl like a cavewoman.

"Lie down on the bed. I'll take care of you."

Josie complied, lying down on the bed Bex laid in. Bex knelt on the soft mattress, a knee on either side of Josie's legs. Her hands cupped those pale, full breasts, squeezing their fullness, thumb and fingers playing with the nipples as Josie made more sexy little moans.

"Please," Josie begged, her legs rubbing together under

Bex, shifting to release some of the pressure Bex was sure was mounting.

Moving her hands slowing down Josie's body, she hooked her fingers into those sleep shorts and tugged.

"Lift up."

Josie complied, lifting her hips so Bex could strip the shorts off and toss them away.

Her eyes fell to the blond curls covering Josie's sex. Her mouth watered, hands gently stroking through their softness.

"I have dental dams," Josie said softly. "In my purse."

She nodded toward her bag across the room. Bex was all for safe sex, but…

"I want to taste you," she confessed.

Josie nodded. "I had my last annual a month ago. All negative. And I haven't been with anyone for six months."

Six months? Seemed like Bex wasn't the only one with a dry spell.

"My annual was two months ago, all clear. And It's been eight months for me."

"I trust you, Bex."

Those words hit something deep within her. Deeper than they should have. This was just supposed to be scratching an itch, fucking away the tension, but Josie's faith in her humbled Bex. She would never take something like that for granted.

"I want to taste you, Josie. Are you okay with that?"

Josie nodded, a shy smile curling her lips. "Yes, please."

Roaring inside, Bex moved down the bed, gently taking Josie's legs and draping them over her shoulders. She kissed one ankle, then the other, repeating the movement all the way up those deliciously long legs until she came to the heaven between them.

Using one hand, she brushed her fingers against Josie's glistening sex, already wet with anticipation.

"Bex!" Josie moaned above her.

Good, but not good enough. Dipping her head, Bex parted Josie with her thumbs and used her tongue to make one long stroke against her. Josie cried out above her, louder this time. Bex chuckled, dipping her tongue inside to taste Josie's sweetness.

"Oh fuck me, Bex. That's amazing."

So, little Miss Sunshine had a dirty mouth in the sack? Bex fucking loved it!

She listened to the sounds Josie made as she used her mouth on her. One hand reached up to press against her stomach as the other found her clit and rubbed soft, slow circles with her thumb. Josie bucked against her face, riding Bex as she sought her pleasure. A pleasure Bex was all too happy to give.

"Bex!" Josie cried out. "More! I need…"

Moving her hand down, Bex moved her mouth up, sucking Josie's clit between her lips while she inserted two fingers inside her.

"Yes!" Josie cried out. "Oh, fuck yes!"

Bex kept up the rhythm, curling her fingers to hit that sweet spot that had Josie's inner walls tightening around her fingers as the woman cried out her release. Bex continues her strokes, gentling Josie with her hand and mouth until she lay sated against the mattress.

"Holy shit, Bex."

She chuckled, climbing up Josie's body to lie beside her. Her own body throbbed, screaming out for release, but she was happy to lie here forever, basking in the glow of the satisfied smile she'd put on Josie's face.

Hazel eyes glanced at her with a hint of challenge in them.

"How do you feel about toys?" Josie asked.

* * *

BEX ROSE ONE DARK BROW. "I'm up for them. Why?"

Josie pressed a quick kiss to her lips, reveling in the fact that she could taste herself on them. She'd never had an orgasm that powerful before. Not even a self-induced one. Bex was some kind of sorcerer.

Which made her all the more anxious to give as good as she got.

"Stay here," she said, scooting off the bed and rushing over to her purse, stumbling a bit as her glasses were still on the nightstand.

"Josie, what are you doing?"

She ignored the question. Rooting around, she squinted as she looked in her bag until she found…yes! There it was.

"Lay back and lose the nightshirt," she commanded.

Bex raised one brow but did as asked.

Josie took a moment to bask in the glory of finally being in the presence of a naked Bex. She was magnificent. No other word for her. Her arms and legs were an intricate patchwork of colorful tattoos. A bit fuzzy looking at the moment. Next time, she'd have to keep her glasses on. Bex's breasts were smaller than Josie's, the nipple slightly darker, and she couldn't wait to taste them. A small landing strip of dark curls ended just above her sex. Josie never would have figured Bex to be one for vag scaping, but she had to admit, it was hot as hell.

"What do you have there?" Bex asked.

Lifting the small black bag in her hand, Josie smiled. She undid the string and dropped the small finger vibrator into her palm.

"You just happened to carry that around in your purse?" Bex asked with a wry smile.

"Never leave home without it," Josie answered.

Bex grinned.

Slipping the device onto her finger, Josie tapped the small button on the end. A soft buzzing sound filled the air. She climbed onto the bed, her empty hand bracing her as she moved her body above Bex's.

"Hi."

Bex smiled. "Hi yourself."

Josie dipped her head, capturing Bex's lips. She would never tire of kissing this woman. Her heart skipped a beat as the warm, honeyed taste of Bex filled her. Warming her in a way no scalding hot shower ever could.

As she devoured Bex's mouth, she moved her hand with the vibrator down Bex's neck to her breasts. A soft moan escaped the woman's lips, and Josie swallowed it down. She moved her finger with the vibrator over one nipple, then the other, teasing the sensitive skin there.

Bex pulled her head back with a small growl. "Fuck, baby, Stop torturing me."

Laughing softly, Josie claimed Bex's mouth once more, moving her hand with the device down Bex's body until it rested between her legs. Bex bucked underneath her. Josie pulled away with a smile as Bex made a sound of protest.

"My turn to taste."

She moved down Bex's body, placing little love kisses along the way until she settled between the other woman's legs. Keeping the toy directly on Bex's clit, she swiped out her tongue, lapping up the wetness gathered there.

'Fuck, Josie!"

She chuckled. "If you say so."

Josie speared Bex with her tongue, keeping the vibrating pressure on her clit as she devoured Bex. Bex's hips pressed against her face, voice calling out above her as her release came hard and fast.

Josie smiled, crawling up her body as Bex's harsh pants filled the air. She clicked the vibrator off and slipped it off her finger, placing it on the nightstand.

"We should get cleaned up," she said.

She started to move off the bed, but Bex's arms came around her, pulling her down into her embrace.

"In a minute," Bex whispered. "Let me hold you for a bit."

Josie nodded, unable to speak. Because Bex didn't realize that if she wanted, Josie would let the woman hold her forever.

CHAPTER 9

*B*ex started up at the ceiling. She had no idea why. Wasn't like she could see much of anything. The room was dark, curtains pulled tight. The only sliver of light came from the soft glow of the dimmed bathroom light.

Even so, she stared.

It had to be close to midnight, maybe even past. The storm had eased. Only a drizzle now as the rain softly pitter-pattered against the window. That was good. What wasn't good was the sinking feeling deep in her gut. The one that screamed at her for what she'd just done.

I slept with Josie!

Her body stiffened as the woman in question snuggled deeper into her arms. Instinctively, she tightened her arm around Josie, pulling her closer and placing a soft kiss to the crown of her head. Josie sighed in her sleep, nuzzling her face against Bex's breast. Her nipples perked up and took notice, but she told her body to calm the hell down. They'd worn each other out. Cleaning up only to go after each other again in the shower and once more when they climbed back into bed. She'd never felt such an intense connection with anyone since…

Ever.

Swallowing down a bit of fear, she pushed away the thought.

She shouldn't be focusing on how amazing Josie made her feel or how delicious she'd tasted, or how much Bex desperately wanted to hear her make those high-pitched little moans of pleasure again.

Fuck, those drove her wild.

What she needed to be focusing on was the fact that she had sex with her best friend's little sister! And all the ramifications of her impulsive action.

Impulsive, ha!

Like she hadn't wanted to do that for years now. Yes, it made her feel like a perv being attracted to Josie, Max's kid sister, but that didn't stop her feelings. But she had been able to control her actions.

Until tonight.

"Mmmmm," Josie's sleep filled voice filled the dark, silent air. "You're worrying too hard. It's waking me up."

"Sorry," she mumbled gruffly, stroking Josie's side with her hand. "I'm fine. Go back to sleep."

"You're not fine."

Josie pushed herself up. Bex wanted to complain, pull the woman back down into her embrace, but with Josie sitting up above her the blanket slipped and even in the dim light she could see the outline of those magnificent breasts she'd had in her mouth only an hour ago. When faced with Josie's breast she could do nothing but stare and worship.

"What's wrong?"

"Huh?" she tried to focus on the question but…boobs.

Josie giggled, grabbing a pillow and softly smacking Bex in the head with it. "Focus, you horndog."

Bex grinned, tossing the pillow back into its spot. Her smile dimmed a bit when Josie tugged the blanket up to cover her naked chest.

Boo.

"Now," the blonde shifted on the bed, grabbing her glasses, and slipping them on before flicking on the bedside light. Bex winced at the brightness. "What's wrong?"

Bex opened her mouth, but she wasn't sure how to put into words all the conflicting emotions rolling around inside her. When she remained silent for too long, Josie's face fell. Her grip on the blanket got tighter as she leaned away.

"Do you regret—"

"No!" Bex sat up, stopping that thought before Josie could finish it. She gripped the other woman's hips and tugged her closer. "I don't regret anything. It was…amazing."

Pale cheeks blush a beautiful pink as a wide smile graced Josie's face. Bex sucked in a sharp breath, the woman's beauty and joy so overwhelming it almost hurt in its splendor.

"I agree, so why do I feel like there's a but coming?"

She frowned, wanting to get her feelings right before she spoke them out loud. Emotions had never been Bex's thing. She wasn't great at them, even if she did experience each and every one in the human range. At this moment, she wished she could be more like Josie, so open and free with how she felt. Bex could never be that brave,

"I guess I'm just wondering and…worried."

Josie's brow furrowed. "Okay, let's take this one thing at a time. First, what are you wondering about?"

She grabbed Josie's hand, stroking her fingers, focusing on the soft, smooth skin, such a contrast to hers. As a welder, Bex's hands were often rough and dirty. Such a difference, and yet when she looked at them together…they fit.

"What are we doing, Josie?" She risked a glance up. Josie smiled an impish little grin.

"Well, until a few minutes ago we were sleeping, at least I was."

"Smartass." She leaned forward, stealing a quick kiss before settling back against the bed's headboard. "No. I mean, was this a one-time thing?"

Josie's smile slipped. "Do you want it to be a one-time thing?"

Hell no!

She wanted more. She wanted everything. But life rarely gave her the things she wanted, so she'd stopped expecting them a while ago. She kept her dreams small and practical. Couldn't be disappointed if you didn't expect much.

"Do you want it to be a one-time thing?" she threw the question back, too afraid to speak her truth.

"Oh no." Josie held up a finger and pointed it. "Don't you do that. Don't you answer my question with the same exact question. What do you want, Bex?"

Dammit, the younger woman was too smart for her own good. She let out a frustrated breath. "It's not as simple as what I want."

"Why not?"

"Max."

Josie frowned. "My brother? What's he got to do with any—"

"Exactly, your brother. My best friend. It's like BFF 101. You don't sleep with siblings."

"We've been over this. Max knows I'm an adult." Hazel eyes stared with purpose. "He doesn't care what I do or who I do it with."

"Yeah, but if…" Her throat started to close up. The words getting stuck, refusing to be spoken into existence for fear of them coming true.

"If what?" Josie moved to lean against the headboard next

67

to Bex, pulling their clasped hands into her lap. "If what, Bex? What has you so worried?"

She turned her head, gaze finding those beautiful hazel eyes, slightly magnified by the lenses of Josie's glasses. Taking a deep breath, she voiced her greatest fear into the night.

"I don't know if I can do more than one night. Because if we start something, *really* start something and it goes south… I'm worried. Worried I'll not only lose you, but Max too. And your parents. My whole—the whole family. I'm not sure I can take that risk."

Her body shook. She'd done it. Said it. Revealed her biggest fear. Just left it out there in the open for Josie to exploit if she wanted. Not that she ever thought the sweet woman would, but fear sometimes made people think irrational things.

"Oh, Bex."

Josie tugged, and she went willingly, allowing herself to be cradled in her lovers' arms, even if it was only for tonight. She'd cherish the memory. Take it out on dark, lonely nights. Remember that for one moment she experienced what true happiness felt like.

"You will never lose my family," Josie whispered in her ear. "Because they're your family too. Always have been."

She sighed. Josie didn't get it. How could she? She didn't know the pain of having your own blood turn you away just for being yourself. Why would Bex ever think her found family wouldn't do the same if she messed with their little girl?

"I know how the world works, Josie," she said, pulling out of the embrace. "Not everything is sunshine and puppies working out perfectly."

One blonde brow rose. "If you think puppies are perfect, you clearly haven't been around enough of them. Those things are tornadoes of trouble."

"You know what I mean."

"I know you're scared."

She scowled, crossing her arms over the blanket covering her chest. "I'm realistic."

"Pessimistic."

The contrary woman was hitting all the points Bex didn't want to see. It was as annoying as it was accurate.

"I'm just stating facts, Josie. What do you think will happen if we start something and things don't work out? Yeah, Max still might be my friend, but when flings end, feelings get hurt, and your brother and parents will take your side every time. As they should, because that's what family is supposed to do."

Understanding filled Josie's eyes. "I wish you had better parents, Bex. You deserve the best. The way they treated you was—"

"This isn't about them." She waved a hand in the air.

"I think it is," Josie insisted. "I think it's always been about them and their rejection. That's not something you just get over. It's a core memory. A wound that never really heals. And it's fucked up they did that to you, but my family? We love you. We'd never toss you aside for any reason."

"I just think it's safer not to start anything that could end in disaster," she mumbled, staring at the bedspread, refusing to look Josie in the eyes. "We had a great night. Maybe we should just leave it at that."

Josie was silent for so long she wondered if the woman went back to sleep, but when she glanced over, she saw hazel eyes staring at her, pain radiating out of them. Aw, fuck! See, they weren't even in a relationship, and she was already hurting Josie. That was the last fucking thing she wanted.

"I don't want to leave it at that," Josie whispered. "I don't want one night. If you're too scared to admit it, I'm not. I want more with you, Bex. I want a relationship. A real one.

One where we're honest with each other, we talk about things, support each other. I want everything."

Damn, she wanted that too. So badly. But she couldn't risk it. Couldn't risk everything when the possibility of them splitting up could ruin everything she had. The family she'd made.

"This isn't just a fling, Bex," Josie continued. "This isn't some one-time weird chemistry we had from being stuck in the car and surviving a scary accident. It isn't adrenalin or some itch we need to scratch. It's real."

"How, Josie?" she asked, trying and failing to keep the worried desperation out of her voice. "How do you know it's real?"

Pale pink lips curved in a soft smile. Josie's hand reached out, cupping Bex's cheek. The warmth of her palm settled some of the racing nerves in her chest. Her eyes fluttered closed as Josie leaned in and placed her lips against Bex's. The kiss was soft and sweet. The taste of her lips imprinted on Bex's very soul. As Josie pulled back, she whispered against Bex's mouth.

"I know it's real, because I love you, Bex."

CHAPTER 10

*J*osie woke up the next morning with a crick in her neck and a pain in her heart. After her impulsive confession last night, Bex muttered something about meeting the tow guy early, rolled over and fell asleep.

Correction, she'd pretended to be asleep. Josie lay awake until the early morning hours, listening to Bex's unsteady breathing. Holding herself tight at the edge of the bed so she didn't disturb the woman who clearly didn't want Josie touching her. She could have moved over to the other bed, but that would have felt too much like giving up. So instead, she lay next to the woman she confessed her love to, mentally berating herself.

Why had she just blurted it out like that?

They just slept together, and she had to go and toss out the big L. Talk about clingy. Bex must be counting the minutes until she could be rid of Josie. She knew spouting off her big feelings would scare the emotionally closed off woman, but she couldn't help herself. Bex kept talking like what they had, what they shared, could be reduced to a fling or one-night stand.

It gutted her.

For Josie, it was more. So much more. Maybe it had been a bad idea to jump into bed with the person she'd been in love with for years.

"Sure was a mistake to say it," she told herself, grateful she was alone in the motel room.

After finally falling asleep with the sun, Josie got in a few hours. When she woke, she glanced around to see no sign of Bex. At first, she'd panicked, thinking Bex ditched her. Only for a second. Then her rational brain caught up with her and reminded her no matter how uncomfortable her confession might have made the other woman, she wouldn't have abandoned Josie like that.

It wasn't in Bex's nature.

Then she'd spied Bex's bag and let out a sigh of relief. Though she'd still been confused. Her confusion had cleared up when she saw a note on the nightstand informing Josie Bex had gone to meet with Sonny and get the car fixed. She had no idea how long the other woman had been gone or when she'd be back. Probably take a few hours by her guess, so she had time to fill.

Yeah, time alone with her thoughts. Just what every person wanted after they confessed their love and were rejected.

Okay, technically, Bex hadn't rejected her. Bex hadn't anything'd her. Other than her sad attempt to change the subject and her laughable fake snores, Bex hadn't said anything to Josie. That could be a good thing, right? She hadn't outright rejected Josie's proclamation of love.

But she hadn't returned it either.

"Ugh! I need coffee."

And a redo of last night. At least the discussion portion of it. She wouldn't erase the earlier events of the night for anything. Repeat them? How she wished she would get a chance to repeat them over and over again.

Josie shuffled over to the window, peeking out the curtains. By the look of the sun, she'd say it was midday. The clock on the nightstand said one. Her stomach grumbled in protest at skipping breakfast.

"Can't get food without a car, buddy," she spoke down to her stomach.

But what she could do was get ready for the day. She didn't know when Bex would be returning, but she figured it would be better to be ready and waiting. A lot better than just sitting here contemplating her life and the events of last night.

Grabbing her bag, she headed to the bathroom to brush her teeth and take care of morning necessities. After swooping her hair up into a ponytail, she washed her face and applied makeup, going into more detail than her usual everyday look. She gave herself a sharp wing and put extra highlighter on her cheekbones. Normally she wouldn't care, but she wanted some armor on for the talk she knew she and Bex had to have. Bex had her badass tattoos and Josie had sparkly eyeshadow and ruby red lipstick.

Just as she finished applying her mascara, she heard the motel room door open. She zipped up her makeup bag and slipped her glasses back on. Staring at her reflection in the mirror, she smiled at a job well done.

Eat your heart out, Bex baby.

"Don't screw this up again," she whispered to her reflection. "Don't freak her out. Talk, but go slow. And no more love confessions."

Her love for Bex hadn't gone anywhere, but clearly it

scared the other woman to hear it, so Josie would hold that in her heart for now. Until Bex was ready to hear it.

She opened the bathroom door to see Bex placing a Styrofoam to-go box and cup on the small round table in the corner of the room.

"Hey," Bex said, adjusting the items on the table before looking up. "I grabbed you some food from the diner near the car shop. There's some coffee and a Denver omelet."

"Thank you, that's my favorite." Josie smiled, trying not to read too much into the food order.

Most roadside places served Denver omelets. They were hard to screw up. Which was why they were Josie's favorite. Just because Bex got her one didn't mean she was specifically remembering they were her favorite breakfast order. She might have just ordered the first thing she saw on the menu.

"I know," Bex said softly.

Josie paused as she opened the food lid. Glancing up, she saw a host of emotions in Bex's eyes. Maybe she was finally ready to talk about—

"You should eat up," Bex said, clearing her throat and quickly crossing to the other side of the room. "We need to hit the road ASAP. Crusher will be pissed if I don't get home in time to give him his weekly strawberry treat tonight."

She sat at the table, digging into the food and holding back a sigh of frustration. Guess Bex wasn't ready to talk. That was fine. Josie could be patient.

Probably.

"The car's fixed?" she asked, shoveling a mouth full of eggs, cheese, and ham into her mouth. Her eyes closed as the savory, salty flavors exploded on her tongue. Her stomach growled in approval, happy it was being sated.

"Yeah. Turns out we hit some metal shit in the middle of the road. Tore the hell out of both tires. Lucky for us, Sonny had replacements on hand. We're good to go."

She grabbed the coffee, taking a small sip before smiling up at Bex. "That's great."

"I'm just gonna go pack the car," Bex said, patting her backpack. "Come on out when you're ready."

Pack the car. Josie snorted as Bex closed the door behind her. More like run away. How damn hard was it to pack a bag into a trunk? Looked like this "patience with Bex" thing was going to be harder than she thought. It seemed Bex didn't want to even acknowledge what Josie said last night. Or anything about last night.

Had they taken one step forward and three steps back?

Josie sighed, finishing the rest of her food and downing her coffee. After a quick stop off in the office to check out and say goodbye to Mabel, they were in the car and back on the road. She'd hoped the intimacy of the car would allow them to discuss things, but the second she got in, Bex cranked up the radio and focused all her attention on the road.

Josie tried not to let it get to her. She understood how her confession freaked out Bex, but her nerves and worry wouldn't let her relax. The car ride home was filled with tension. Not even the upbeat rock songs playing on the car radio pulled her out of her funk. She'd messed up. Maybe so much that this thing was unrepairable.

Dammit! She knew better. She knew Bex didn't like to discuss emotional stuff, but Josie had never been that way. She told people how she felt. Always. It had never been a problem. Until now.

They made it to Woodland Hills without another incident. A fact she'd be much happier about if her heart wasn't currently ripping apart.

As they pulled into the half circle driveway for the duplex, Josie felt her emotions overwhelm her. Max sat on the front porch between his door and her new place. He waved, a big smile on his face. There he sat. Her brother. The man she had to thank and curse for her current situation. It wasn't Max's fault he had an emergency yesterday which facilitated Bex picking her up instead, snowballing this whole damn mess into what it was now.

But she was sitting here, holding back tears, inches away from the woman she loved, feeling miles separating them, because he hadn't been able to pick her up. Maybe the price of a rideshare would have been easier.

On her heart anyhow.

She glanced over to see Bex staring at Max, fear in her eyes. That's when it really hit her. Bex's fear, her hesitation. Josie really didn't understand where Bex was coming from because, well, because she'd never experienced a loss like Bex's. Josie's family had been great when she came out. She didn't even really need to. They'd always just accepted her as she was. Bex didn't have that. Josie would never know the pain of losing someone who was supposed to love you unconditionally.

It didn't erase the pain from her heart, but it did help her understand where the other woman was coming from. And even if it killed her to do so, she realized she couldn't force Bex to talk about things if she wasn't ready to. Josie had to accept the possibility that Bex might never be ready to.

Swallowing down her tears, she cleared her throat and spoke softly.

"We don't have to talk about it if you don't want to. Last night," she clarified. "No one has to know. We can just go on like we always have. I understand, Bex. Really, I do."

Silence filled the car. After a beat or two, Josie held back a sigh and reached for the door handle. As she moved to step out of the car, Bex's low voice made her pause.

"Did you mean it?"

She turned back to glance at the woman. Bex was staring at her lap, fiddling with the car keys.

"Did you mean what you said about…loving me?"

"Yes," she whispered, afraid to say it too loudly and scare her again. "I love you, Bex. I have for a long time. I was waiting for you to see it, see me. Not as Max's sister, but as my own person."

Bex glanced up, eyes shimmering with unshed tears. "I do see you. You're an amazing woman, Josie. Smart, funny, kind, beautiful. Too fucking good for me, that's for sure."

"Don't say that." She reached over, grabbing Bex's hands. The other woman obliged, dropping her keys and holding on tight. "You are amazing, Bex. You're so strong and clever. You're generous, always willing to lend a hand. You don't judge people and you always try to do the right thing, even if it's at a sacrifice to your own happiness."

A tear fell down Bex's cheek. Josie brushed it away with her thumb.

"I love you, Bex, but I understand if you don't love me or are too scared of losing—"

"I do," Bex whispered, her eyes widening as if she couldn't believe the words that fell out of her lips.

Josie sucked in a sharp breath, too afraid to read into those two words without clarification. "What?"

"I…I love you too, Josie. I tried not to. I was scared you might not love me back, or I'd screw everything up, and your brother would have to kick my ass."

She laughed. "Please, I'd bet you could kick Max's ass up and down the street."

Bex smiled, a real, genuine, full watt mega smile. The sight stole Josie's breath away.

"I didn't want to hurt anyone, most of all you. I guess I just never imagined you could ever love me too."

"Well, I do." She shifted over in her seat, cupping Bex's

face in her hands. "And I know life isn't perfect. People fight, tires get blown, hotel rooms come with two beds when they should only come with one for romantic purposes."

Bex laughed.

"But I know that when you love someone, you share with them. All your hopes and your fears and you work through things together. Think we can do that?"

Bex nodded. "Yeah. I think we can."

"Me too."

Bex grasped the back of her neck, pulling her closer. She pressed her mouth against Josie's, tongue pressing against the seam of her lips, demanding entrance. She readily complied. Bex deepened the kiss, drinking her in. She loved it. Loved her. Her heart soared as happiness filled every single ounce of her body.

"I love you, Josie." Bex said as she pulled away, pressing their foreheads together.

"I love you too."

She stepped out of the car, smile so wide her cheeks hurt. But it was a good hurt. A happy one. One she never wanted to go away. Bex rounded the car and grabbed her hand, lacing their fingers together as they walked up to the front of the duplex. Max sat there in the front porch rocker, smiling at them. His gaze went to their hands, the car, then their hands again.

Standing, he grinned at both of them. "Finally! I thought you two would never wise up and get your act together."

"What are you talking about?" Bex said, her brow furrowed in confusion.

Max gave her a droll look. "Come on, Bex. I've known you had a thing for my sister for years now."

Bex's jaw dropped, her cheeks turned red as she stumbled over her words. "What? How could you...what do you..."

"He's pretty observant," Josie said, smiling at her brother.

Max gave her another pointed look. "And I know you've been over the moon about my best friend since high school, Jojo."

She shrugged. Why argue with the truth?

"I'm just glad you both finally admitted it, but keep the PDA to a minimum around the sibling, please. I don't need any of that haunting me at night."

Bex tugged her close, dipping Josie and planting a big, wet, deep kiss on her lips.

"Oh come on, Bex!" Max complained. "What did I just say?"

Josie giggled against Bex's lips, giving her brother her middle finger.

"You're both assholes. I rescind my offer to make dinner tonight."

"Okay, okay," Josie said, ending the kiss and standing. "We're sorry. And exhausted from the trip, please make us dinner."

Max laughed, ushering them inside, telling her he'd help her get settled in a few. She followed her brother, stopping when Bex tugged on her hand.

"What's up?" she asked, watching her brother disappear inside. "You're staying for dinner, right?"

"Yeah, I just wanted another kiss, a real one. Not one to gross out your brother."

A real kiss from Bex. There was nothing better in the world. She'd give this woman a hundred kisses if she wanted. A million. So many, even the best mathematicians in the world wouldn't be able to count them.

"For you, my love." She grinned. "Anything."

"And for you," Bex pulled her close, head lowering as their mouths hovered centimeters apart. "Everything."

Josie smiled as her lover claimed her lips.

Anything and everything. That's what they meant to each

other, that's what they could handle. Because they had each other. Life could throw them all the curveballs in the world. All the flat tires and flash floods, but they'd see it through. Together. Because they had love and they had each other.

Sounded just about perfect to her.

The End

ABOUT THE AUTHOR

Bestselling author Mariah Ankenman lives in the beautiful Rocky Mountains with her two rambunctious children and loving spouse who is her own personal spell checker when her dyslexia gets the best of her.

Mariah loves to lose herself in a world of words. Her favorite thing about writing is when she can make someone's day a little brighter with one of her books. To learn more about Mariah and her books head her to her website: https://mariahankenman.com/ or follow her on social media @mariahankenman. To stay up to date on all her releases and sales sign up for her newsletter.

ALSO BY MARIAH